balloons

necklace

brush

ponies

butterflies

pony

cake

prize

castle

ribbons

clock

star

crown

wind

kite

Belle of the Ball

by Ruth Benjamin

illustrated by Ken Edwards

HarperFestival®
A Division of HarperCollinsPublishers

The  were excited

about the Best Friends' Ball.

Twinkle Twirl was busy

at the dance studio.

Sweetberry was busy

baking a .

At the ,

the worked hard.

They blew up .

They tied the

with shiny .

Skywishes left the 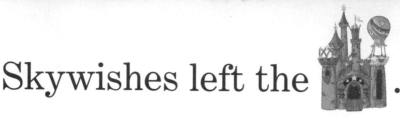.

She stopped to visit

Twinkle Twirl.

"Do you want to fly a

with me?" asked Skywishes.

"I can't now,"

said Twinkle Twirl.

"I am teaching the

a new dance."

"I will leave the 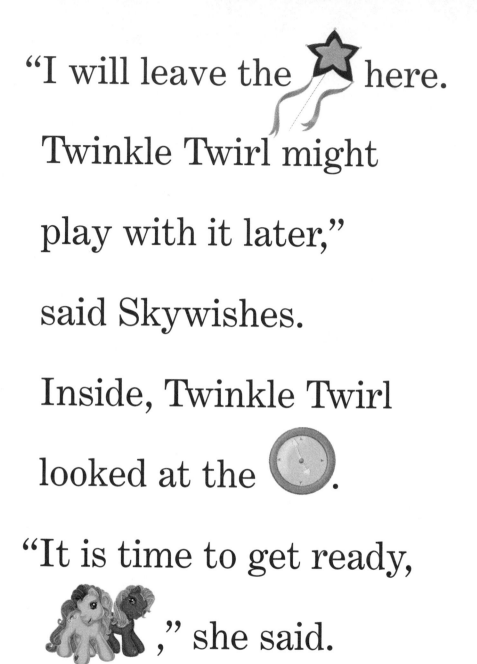 here.

Twinkle Twirl might

play with it later,"

said Skywishes.

Inside, Twinkle Twirl

looked at the ⏱.

"It is time to get ready,

🐴," she said.

"May I wear your 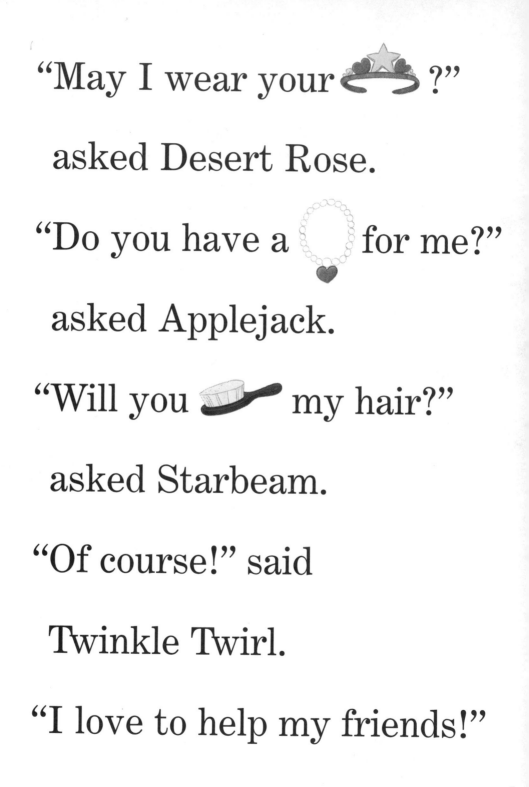 ?"

asked Desert Rose.

"Do you have a ⬡ for me?"

asked Applejack.

"Will you 🖌 my hair?"

asked Starbeam.

"Of course!" said

Twinkle Twirl.

"I love to help my friends!"

It was time for

Twinkle Twirl to get ready.

She had no .

She had no .

She had no one to

her hair.

How could she go

to the ball?

Twinkle Twirl looked up

at the .

Skywishes' was

flying in the .

"A wishing star!" she said.

"I wish I had a

and a .

Then I could go to the ball."

"Your wishes *will* come true,"

said a pretty .

 were all around him.

"My name is ⭐ Catcher."

"Wow!" said Twinkle Twirl.

"You are a real

pegasus ."

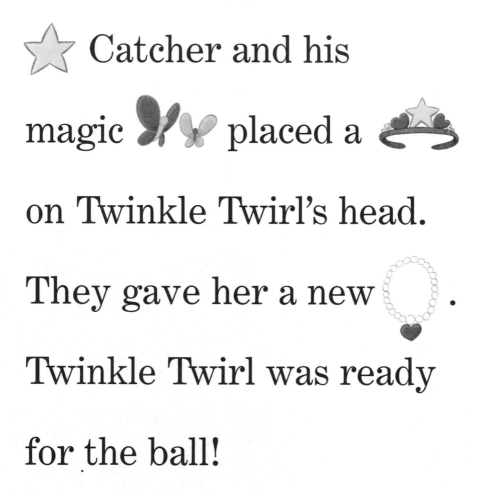 Catcher and his

magic placed a

on Twinkle Twirl's head.

They gave her a new .

Twinkle Twirl was ready

for the ball!

Twinkle Twirl went

to the 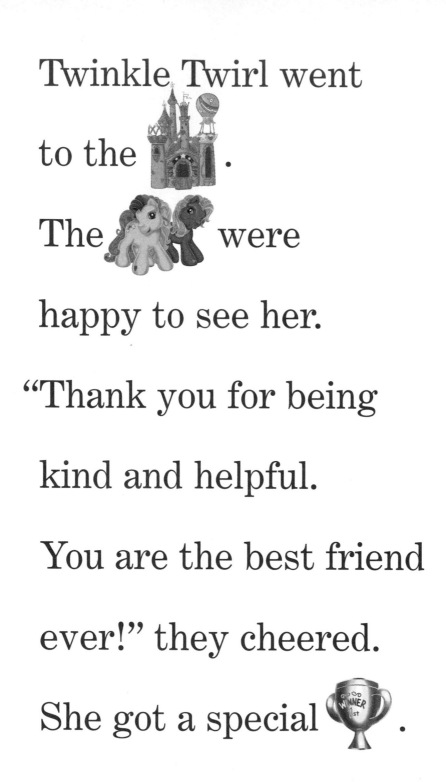.

The 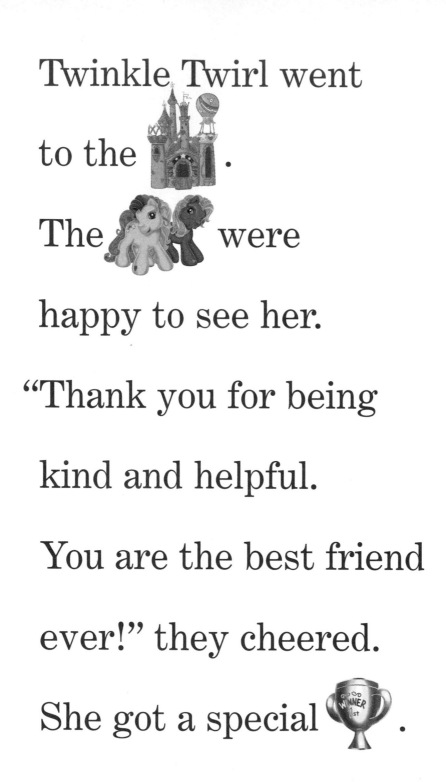 were

happy to see her.

"Thank you for being

kind and helpful.

You are the best friend

ever!" they cheered.

She got a special 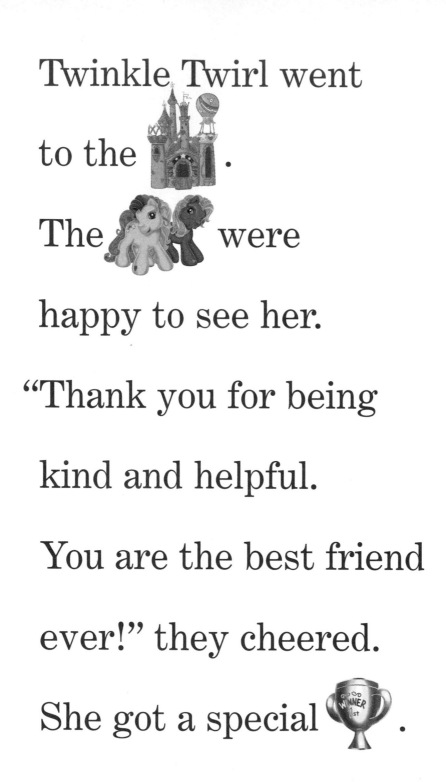.

Twinkle Twirl was

the ⭐ of the ball.

But the best part of all was

being with good friends–

best friends forever!